EVEN DICTATORS NEED DOGS

STORIES & POEMS

HENRY F. ZACCHINI

ONION RIVER PRESS

BURLINGTON, VERMONT

Onion River Press
191 Bank Street
Burlington, VT 05401

ISBN: 978-1-957184-09-8
Library of Congress Control Number: 2022912624

For My Father and His Grandchildren Who Loved Him

God speaks to each of us as he makes us,
then walks with us silently out of the night.
These are the words we dimly hear:
You, sent out beyond your recall,
go to the limits of your longing.
Embody me.
Flare up like a flame

and make big shadows I can move in.
Let everything happen to you: beauty and terror.
Just keep going. No feeling is final.
Don't let yourself lose me.
Nearby is the country they call life.
You will know it by its seriousness.
Give me your hand.

– RAINER MARIA RILKE

ACKNOWLEDGEMENTS

This book would not have been possible without the love and support of many family and friends. I would like to thank my wife, Rachel. She has been a tower of strength and love in my life. My children, Quinn and Amelia, make me proud every day and inspire me to write. To my mother Sharon and sister Larissa, you've helped mold the person I am. To my many editors including Greg Joly, Jodi Berggren, Rachel Glickman, and Sharon Matzek, thank you. This book would have been impossible without your help. To Andy West, the remarkable designer of this book (and all my other books) and lifelong friend. We walked to school together as youngsters and are now walking together in middle age. To Rachel Fisher at Onion River press. It's nice to have a local Vermont publisher to work with.

CONTENTS

INTRODUCTION

The beautiful thing about publishing your own work is that you can do whatever you like. The downside, of course, is that few people will read what you have spent years composing. Since I am not writing to make a living, nor to put food on the table, a paucity of readers is a small price to pay for the joy and necessity of writing as I like. This book spans several years of my life and includes both poems and short stories, some of which are about death and others which are not, aside from the fact that perhaps everything is about death. Over the past couple of years, I have lost people who were dear to me, including my father. The idea and reality of loss carries weight for the living; the dead are elsewhere. We are left here to muddle through, to make sense of the world without the decedent's active presence in our lives. One way, at least for me, to reconcile this predicament is to write.

Two of these stories, "Kenzo in Oxford" and "Zombies in Hillingdon," were inspired, at least loosely, by my time living in England. I found the alienation palpable while living there, so if there is a theme in these two stories, perhaps it is that. To be fair, I've found alienation in other places as well. The story about zombies was completed well before the current pandemic began, but the connection is there. After these horrifying and perilous years, I'm not sure the world needs another zombie apocalypse story, but I wanted to write one, so here it is. The third story, "A Cleansing," was inspired by my fascination with the United States' merciless foreign policy in Latin America and the impact this has had on the countries that experienced these outrages.

As for the poems, many are about death, some about the living trying to make sense of death and dying, others about love and dogs. Beyond this, it is best to let the poems fend for themselves.

SECTION ONE:
KENZO IN OXFORD

SCENE ONE: ON HIS WAY

His mother cried at his departure. Kenzo was not sure if they were tears of sadness or pride, but she was a mess. His father, being traditionally Japanese, was largely emotionless, although he did smile, which was rare enough. His younger sister just pointed and laughed and gave him a big hug before he left them standing, mouths agape, in the airport lounge.

God the fucking flight was long. Flying from Tokyo to London without stopping was madness. Being stuck in a metal tube with fake air, bad movies, uncertain smells, eating odd, disgusting food, interspersed with terror-inducing turbulence, was completely nuts. He walked around the aisles in big circles, occasionally talking up a steward or stewardess in Japanese or English depending on whom he ran into. This pattern made some of the other passengers uncomfortable until they fell asleep, then he walked around mostly unnoticed.

He experienced an overwhelming feeling of relief as soon as the plane left Japan. His little prefecture on the outskirts of Tokyo had not been a good match. He'd done very well at school, as his parents expected him to, and his classmates always liked him, even if they considered him somewhat odd and treated him as if he were Gaijin. His choice of school confused his friends. Why go to England for university? What was the point? It was so far away and there were so many good schools in Japan.

His family had been on the island for millennia. They were so Japanese he'd had the crazy thought that his ancestors might have already been on Honshu before the other ancient migrants arrived and had probably helped get them acquainted with how things worked on the island. He'd heard stories that his family was related to the imperial family, that his great, great, great grandfather had been a samurai and that his great grandmother had been a concubine to the emperor. They were all lies for sure, yet these delusions of grandeur had, to some degree, shaped his and his family's perception of themselves.

He was done with it. Done with the bullshit, the culture, the silence, the hidden suffering. It was time to move on, to be anywhere different. He was, especially given the awfulness of the plane ride, seriously considering never returning. Japan to him was like a lunatic asylum where everyone, as they suffered repeated existential crises, remained calm and pretended everything was normal.

Ultimately, he was odd enough to leave. His English was impeccable, and he was sure that Oxford and England were just where he needed to be.

SCENE TWO: DISNEY WORLD

He had never been to Disney World, but he'd heard stories and was sure that he had somehow ended up in a version of it even if Oxford was supposed to be a serious university. When he thought about life, it often occurred to him that much of existence was this way. There was the stated, universally believed truth about something or someone, and the unstated, actual reality. Oxford was very much this way. Although he was a nonconformist by Japanese standards, he'd fully expected that he would lead a regular student life at Oxford. He would major in English and mathematics at Christ Church, as he'd promised. However, because school came so easily to him, he also planned to embrace his new life and fill it with as many experiences as he could. He felt literally and figuratively, for the first time in his life, untethered. His attitude towards and approach to his new life changed a bit once he realized what was happening at Christ Church.

He arrived on a typical blustery English day at the end of September, with the plan of finding his dormitory room and getting acquainted with the town. He had not checked in with the college staff about his arrival time, but he figured he could just find the housing office after he landed.

The bus dropped him off on the high street in the middle of a throng of people. He knew there were tourists in Oxford, but he could not fully believe what he was seeing. Groups of Asian and pasty White tourists heading every direction, some taking pictures, others reading maps, still others being led by tour guides; what a spectacle. While the buildings certainly were old and beautiful, the tourists caught his primary attention.

Once he got his bearings, he walked to Christ Church to find the housing office. He had a hard time locating the entrance, so he skirted around the outside of the complex until he saw a long line of people waiting to get into the buildings. They were all tourists, many of whom had come to the college to see the dining room, which had been used for inspiration in creating one of the Harry Potter movies' sets. Even though he knew he didn't have to, he decided to wait in line with them.

After about an hour, he arrived at the ticket counter.

"Hello, I'm not here for the Harry Potter tour. I'm a new student and I'm looking for the housing office."

The woman in the booth looked confused. "Sorry love I didn't hear you."

"Yes, I'm a new student and I'm looking for the housing office."

She was still uncertain. "A student?"

"I'm a Christ Church student and I need to speak with the housing office to find my room," he said politely in his best British accent.

"Oh love, you didn't need to wait in this line—sorry. I'm not actually certain where the housing office is. I just work in the ticket office, but I could ring someone up. No, better yet, just head into the main square and look for one of the guards. They should be able to help you." She smiled at him through the glass.

He walked into the main part of the grounds on the heels of dozens of tourists with cameras. The buildings were quite impressive. Old, imposing, tan-brick classical style buildings with beautiful vines growing up their walls, accompanied by lovely flower beds and a grand stairway beckoning the tourists towards the main dining hall where they could view, according to the sign at the ticket booth, "The room that inspired the dining hall in the Harry Potter films."

The tourist path eventually led to the college's famous quadrangle, a large open space with sculpted, impossibly green lawns and more gaping, picture-taking tourists. The quadrangle was rimmed by a concrete walkway. He spied a man in a blue jacket on the far side of the square who looked as though he might be a guard. As Kenzo approached him, the man began waving his arms and shouting something that Kenzo could not hear. At that moment Kenzo heard another person yelling from his right and realized that two officials in blue jackets were coming towards him from different directions.

He now could hear what the man approaching from the front was saying: "Excuse me, excuse me! Can't you read the sign? You're not allowed in this part of the grounds. Please turn around. Thank you."

Not sure what his next move should be, Kenzo stood in place.

"Yes, you sir, please turn around and head back to where you came from."

The guard was now only fifteen feet in front of him but was speaking in a volume just below yelling. The guard was still waving his arms over his head like a man directing a jet, perhaps under the assumption that Kenzo spoke very little English and thus would understand better with non-verbal cues.

"Hello," Kenzo started, "I'm a new student from Japan and the woman in the ticket booth told me that you could help me find the housing office."

The man stopped in his tracks a few feet in front of him. "Sir you've got to... What?" The guard looked puzzled.

Some of the tourists around the quad had stopped pointing their cameras at the buildings and started looking at Kenzo and the guards.

"I'm a new Christ Church student. I'm searching for the housing office," Kenzo said loudly; he was unsure what volume to use given the distance the guard was standing away from him.

The guard chuckled, "Ok mate, you're a bit in the wrong place. You've got to go through that doorway on the other side of the quad."

As he walked towards the housing office, Kenzo felt a sense of joy. He was excited about starting his new life in England.

SCENE THREE: HAIRCUT

His first months at Oxford ended up being different than he'd hoped. When he left Japan, he was sure that he was leaving his old life behind, including the parts of Japanese social culture that he could no longer tolerate. He was tired of the insularity and the conformity and loved the idea of avoiding his parents' constant haranguing.

Nonetheless, he found life in England perplexing, with some eerie similarities to life in Japan. Both countries prided themselves on tradition and both were full of people (at least it seemed to him) who were staunchly chauvinistic about their place of birth. He'd thought it had something to do with being denuded, imperialistic island nations. It was as if the beating both countries took during the last world war had had the opposite effect of what one might expect. Instead of humbling the peoples' sense of themselves in the world, the losses served to merely enhance entrenched feelings of cultural superiority. It was not that Kenzo did not appreciate what Japan and England had achieved from such small beginnings—he loved stories about underdogs—it was just that his move to England was peppered with experiences that reminded him of why he'd left his home country. Still, Kenzo felt that experiencing another country's contradictions was highly preferable to experiencing the contradictions of his own.

He also found that he was surprised by his reaction to these dawning revelations. While most of his Asian classmates got busy with their studies as soon as they disembarked from their *Get to Know England* boat trip on the Thames, he found himself staring out windows during classes looking for new species of birds or wandering around Oxford late at night once all of the students and tourists had gone to bed. He began to sleep late, started to miss more classes than he attended, and was getting a little fat as he industriously plowed through his portion of British beer and cheese.

When he spent time thinking about his life in Japan it led to small epiphanies. One of these thought processes caused him to let his hair grow longer. He'd often felt jealous of the young punks with crazy hair he saw when he took trips into the center of Tokyo. He'd wanted so badly to do something outrageous with his hair, but he knew his parents would disown him, so he was left looking. While he realized the punks' getups were simply a different sort of conformity, they were at least pushing back against Japanese society in some small way. He now wanted to push back too,
so when a classmate joked that Kenzo should dye his hair bright red, he agreed and went to the hairdresser the very next day.

His hairdresser was a local English woman in her early twenties with the thick accent of the British working class, which he loved. She had multiple tattoos and piercings in her nose and mouth to go along with the ones in her ears. She was confused about his request.

"You want what?" she said, looking puzzled.

"Could you please dye my hair orange with some small black dots?" Kenzo smiled amiably.

"Um, what?"

"Yes, I would like you to dye my hair orange with some black leopard spots," Kenzo said more slowly. This time he pointed to his head while he spoke, as if he were applying the spots himself.

"Oh love, you don't want to do such a thing. You've got lovely hair, just the way it is." She chuckled a bit.

In the end, he succeeded in convincing her he needed the hairstyle for a play he was going to be in. There was no play, but he got the hair. He couldn't have been more pleased with it.

SCENE FOUR: A CALL TO JAPAN

His parents insisted on speaking with him every week. This requirement was becoming harder and harder for him to manage. It would have been one thing if they'd simply wanted a five-minute chat over the phone, but that was never enough. His mother insisted they talk via video chat. Seeing him made them concerned. He knew he looked different now that he'd been in England for a couple of months, although he could not be sure what they perceived. He was fairly certain that they were catching onto his lack of studying because every time they asked him about his classes, he just changed the subject or refused to answer. This was partially because he found talking about school very boring, but also because he was spending less and less time in the classroom. He'd been able to put them off for a couple of weeks after he got his new hairstyle, but he finally decided to show them.

His mother screamed and ran away from the video camera when she saw him. She yelled for his father, "Hiroki, Hiroki, go look at your son!"

Kenzo was left staring at the white wall of their living room, but he could hear his mother sobbing in the background.

His father sat down in front of the camera and looked at him, expressionless. They sat there not speaking, staring at each other, thousands of miles apart. After several minutes, which seemed like an eternity to Kenzo, the connection went dead. He was pretty sure his father had hung up on him.

SCENE FIVE: HELLMUND

Most of his classes were incredibly tedious. He was enthusiastic about his English literature class, though, not so much due to the content, or the readings (which he did not read), but due to his oddball professor. He'd heard about eccentric British people during his studies in Japan, but nothing prepared him for Professor Hellmund. Hellmund was a middle-aged man with graying, profoundly unkempt hair who wore clothing to match. He would often arrive to class twenty minutes to a half hour late, which Kenzo valued. Kenzo would sit and watch as the other students became more and more irritated at their professor's lack of promptness. They waited, of course, because they knew what Kenzo knew: no matter how long you had to wait, you should; Hellmund always put on a show.

The professor would enter the room mumbling to himself and then stop once he arrived at his desk and look up at the class as if to say, "Ah yes, let's continue."

His talks were so esoteric and so tangential that, ten minutes into the lecture, Kenzo often had no idea what the beginning thread had been. The professor would barely touch upon the book they were supposed to have read and would instead be off, connecting some bird species he had seen on a boat trip down the Niger River to the comic genius of Oscar Wilde. Kenzo never took notes in Hellmund's class, he just sat staring at the mad genius in front of him, letting his mind wander along with the professor's, sometimes paying attention sometimes not.

When students attempted to ask a question or made an effort to bring the class back to the literature at hand, Hellmund would start, as if woken from a dream and say, "Yes, right. What pages have you read since I last saw you?"

SCENE SIX: A BICYCLE

He loved biking but had never really been given the chance to ride much in Japan. Even though most of his friends biked throughout the suburb where he lived, his mother thought that biking was dangerous. He had learned to bike by borrowing friends' bikes; she let him get a bike on his eleventh birthday. Still, she tried to do what she could to limit the amount of riding he did. Before he left for England, he vowed that his first purchase would be a used bike.

He was overjoyed to discover that bicycles in Oxford were cheap and plentiful. It was a particularly surprising discovery because everything else in England was very expensive. At first, he looked online and then learned from friends that there was an excellent used bike shop just outside of the town center. The store was owned and operated by an elderly Scot.

The Scotsman was a little confused about what kind of bike Kenzo was looking for.

"You want a bike with streamers?" Kenzo wanted a colorful, outrageous bike.

"Yes, that's correct," Kenzo said. "I'm looking for a colorful bike with streamers and preferably a basket on the front."

The shop owner was confused. "Well, we've got a woman's bike in the back that might fit you. It's bright pink with purple wheels and a purple basket."

It fit him perfectly, so he bought the bike. He loved it. It also had a purple bell with a butterfly on it that he liked to ding at the tourists as he rode through town.

SCENE SEVEN: PUNTING

He knew from early in his days at Christ Church that the college would not be able to fully keep his interest. He also realized it would limit the kinds of experiences he wished to have in England. When he thought about ways he could more fully grasp his new life, he decided that he needed to give employment a try. It would serve the dual purpose of getting him out of the school into the larger community and providing him the chance to meet new people. He also thought that his language skills might come in handy, given the number of Asian tourists wandering through the city.

His first idea for employment was the punting boats. Punting boats were the English version of Venetian canal boats. They were also ground zero for the Oxford tourists. They descended on the punting docks in droves, especially when the weather was nice. He knew some of the punting outfits hired university students because several of his older classmates had been punters during the summer months. The college punters were paid very little, unless they were able to finagle tips. He figured he could make very big tips based on his language skills alone. The Asian tourists would be glad to see an Asian boat driver and the anglophone tourists would marvel at his proper British accent and silly hair.

The man who ran the punting boats closest to the college was a grumpy, paunchy middle-aged Englishman named Charlie. Kenzo had watched Charlie on several occasions from the bridge above the boat launch and knew that Charlie spent quite a bit of time berating his punters as soon as the tourists left the dock, so Kenzo approached with some caution.

"Hello," Kenzo said in his most proper British accent. "I'd like to drive your punting boats."

"Well mate, that'll be 15 quid if you're alone or 25 quid with a driver," Charlie said, ignoring Kenzo's proclamation.

"No thank you," Kenzo said politely. "My name is Kenzo and I want to work for you."

"My name is Charlie and I don't make a habit of hiring foreigners to run my boats, especially those with polka dot hair."

Kenzo persisted in a courteous voice, "But you can pay me on the side. I just want a chance to meet people, to see the river, and make a few tips. I know you've hired other students before. I promise to wear a hat."

"So you've heard, have ya," Charlie chuckled at him. "Well, you won't see much of the river from here. Most of the boats don't make it even part way to the Thames. You're a tad slender to run the boats."

Kenzo felt he was making progress. "If you give me the chance you will see that I am strong enough. I will also help with all of your Japanese tourists."

Charlie looked amused. "OK then, come back tomorrow with a hat and some smarter clothes and we'll give it a go."

Kenzo returned the next day wearing his nicest pants and shirt, and a hat on his head. Charlie gave him a few basic instructions about punting and then handed him the punting pole. Charlie and his two regular punters stood on the dock and watched as Kenzo pushed the boat from the dock. He realized the second he put the pole in the water that punting was more challenging than he'd thought. It was difficult for him to gauge how hard to push the pole without compromising his upright position at the rear of the boat. After about fifteen minutes on the canal he was able to return the boat to the dock. Based on his level of exertion on his solo ride, he was worried about the prospect of pushing a whole family through the canals. But he'd enjoyed the short trip. The sun was breaking through the clouds as they spit out the occasional rain shower. Birds were fluttering to their nests along the canal, and families walking on the adjacent towpath had smiled and waved at him as he floated by.

"OK," Charlie said, "We've got a Japanese group set for the 11 o'clock spot. Are you ready?"

Kenzo was not at all sure he was ready, but he assured Charlie that he was, "Yes, I am very excited."

The Japanese group consisted of a mother and father, an older grandmother and a boy and a girl both under the age of ten. It was clear that he would have to take them on one of the larger punting boats. They seemed confused and hesitant about the prospect of having a Japanese punter, perhaps expecting to be piloted by a full-blooded Englishman like Charlie. To ease their hesitancy, he immediately started to speak with them in Japanese about the wonders of Oxford and began to describe what they would see on their tour (which he largely made up). They loaded themselves unsteadily into their seats.

The beginning of the trip went fine, even if the boat was a bit difficult to manage. When he'd seen the gondolas of Venice on television, the drivers were always so serene and well-dressed. He felt neither serene nor well-dressed and was finding that it took most of his strength to guide the boat down the canal in a straight line. At one point the whole family had to duck because Kenzo brought the boat too close to the trees overhanging the shore. Some people on the towpath were looking upon Kenzo's group with amusement, which, when he thought about it later, seemed reasonable. He was sweating quite profusely and felt the need to take his hat off, so his hair was now on full display. He was almost yelling at his passengers in Japanese. He hadn't meant to speak so loudly, but the combination of his exertion and the grandmother complaining that she was missing the tour commentary forced him to raise his voice. He was just speaking nonsense because he did not know what they were looking at; he'd not spent much time on Oxford history since his arrival.

Even so, by the time they approached the dock again he was feeling pretty good about his first tour and imagined that the family might hand him a fiver for his troubles. The last obstacle before their homecoming was a low-slung walking bridge with a tunnel that crossed the canal right before the dock. As Kenzo navigated the short tunnel, the bottom of his punting pole got stuck in the mud at the base of the canal and the top part of his pole caught the arch of the bridge almost simultaneously. He tried desperately to hang onto his pole, but it pulled him out of the boat. He screamed as he fell and instinctively grabbed the side of the boat, which sent the family into the canal with him.

His scream was unwarranted as the canal was only three feet deep where they capsized. He never captained another punting boat and didn't get a fiver for a tip. In the end, he thought the experience was worthwhile. He realized Charlie and the wet Japanese tourists might not have agreed.

SCENE EIGHT: ECONOMICS

Oh god, Kenzo thought, there she goes again babbling on about utils. Even though he'd not taken his academic pursuits seriously since arriving at Christ Church, he'd not lost his proclivity for scientific thought. It was one of the traits that he prided himself on—being able to look at the world through a dispassionate, analytical lens—but this woman was too much. For the past week, Professor Bradley, his middle-aged, undernourished British economics instructor with bad skin and thinning hair, who clearly had never run any sort of business and appeared to have been an academic since her preschool years, had been discussing the microeconomic concept of "utils" with the class. He'd had enough. It was clear to him, as a non-economist, that the subject was calcified and laden with myths that simply got passed from one generation of economics professors to the next, with little thought about what was really happening on earth. While he in no way considered himself knowledgeable about the world's problems, he at least understood that humanity was living under a broken economic system.

"Excuse me, could you please tell me what the real value of a util is and how it can be measured among an entire population?" He knew the question had no answer. Kenzo was sure that utils—supposedly a metric to measure the satisfaction a person derives from consumption—must have been created by an economist who'd never seen the light of day.

The professor, looking a bit stunned, stood for a moment at the head of the class and tried to make sense of the question. "Excuse me Kenzo?"

Kenzo repeated the question as he'd asked it. Now the other students in the class, some of whom had clearly drifted away from the monotonous lesson, began to pay attention.

"Well, Kenzo," she said, in a condescending tone, "it's just a theoretical construct that economists use to evaluate satisfaction and consumption. It is not intended to be a scientific formula. It is simply a model to help explain how individual people act when given real economic choices. Utils are not used to look broadly across society. They are a microeconomic rather than macroeconomic tool." The professor seemed pleased with her response and smiled at Kenzo.

"Forgive me for disagreeing professor but talking about utils seems about as useful as discussing monkeys flying airplanes. Perhaps we should also spend time in class talking about the possibility of trading goods with creatures from the center of the earth." Several of the students in the class snickered. One student spit out a mouthful of water.

Professor Bradley's face turned bright pink. "As I said," replying with exasperation, "utils are just a theory to help us think about how people behave when given choices of consumption. And they…"

"Utils are bullshit and so is most of what we're learning in this class," Kenzo interrupted in a loud voice. He no longer felt like being polite. A couple of the students whistled when he raised his voice and a few others turned in their seats to throw him nasty stares.

"Kenzo that is incredibly rude," she said quietly. "If you don't want to be here, at least have the decency to let the other students learn without distractions."

That was all he needed. He picked up his bag and walked out of the classroom. He was looking forward to being outside; it was a sunny day by British standards, and he'd been inside all morning.

SCENE NINE: ADVICE

Kenzo's advisor had a smile on his face when they met outside of his office. "Come in Kenzo," he said. "Let's talk."

Cecil Barnes was slightly past middle age and had worked at Christ Church for his entire professional career. Kenzo had heard rumors that Barnes was once a potential future star of the college, but that did not fit Kenzo's impression of who the man was. Barnes was an affable sort of person who got on well with students and his
colleagues, taught his classes and kept his head down. The "heavy hitters" who worked at Oxford carried themselves very differently than Barnes. Most of them seemed as intent on creating a persona as they did on teaching; Barnes gave no indication of trying to impress anyone.

"Kenzo you really can't continue making a scene in your classes," Barnes started, with a chuckle. "I mean, calling out Professor Bradley in her classroom, using profanities, getting the other students' hackles up. Is there something we need to talk about? Are you happy here?"

"Professor Barnes, have you ever studied economics?"

"I'm not sure," Barnes replied. "I might have taken a class at university, but that was a long time ago."

"It's just not a serious subject," Kenzo started. "It's as if a few economists in the world got together and made some things up, and then the rest of the economists just said, 'Well that sounds as good as anything.' I can't take it. Isn't this supposed to be a real academic institution?"

"Well, Kenzo, according to almost every other institution of higher learning in the world, Oxford is very much a real academic institution." Barnes smiled. "Plus, it's very hard for me to believe that you are accessing the full Christ Church experience, because, based on what you've told me, you have spent as much time not attending your classes as you have attending them."

"I can't do it," Kenzo replied, ignoring what Barnes said. "I like my classmates, but they are churning out the work so that they can graduate and fall in line." Kenzo laid it out: "I'm tired of getting dressed up for dinner. I'm tired of all those stuffy old White men glaring down at me from their portraits as I eat. It's almost like they're pointing fingers at me, wondering why I'm here. I guess they're right because I'm wondering too. Anyway, I've discussed this with my parents and they both agree that I should take some time off to explore England and get my head on straight." His parents could not have disagreed more, but they were thousands of miles away.

"Kenzo, you're in the middle of the term—perhaps you should just let this idea settle and then re-evaluate your situation at the end of the school year. I also think that you have great potential as a scholar." Based on his pained facial expression when he said it, Barnes clearly had little hope in Kenzo's academic potential.

"You will also forfeit all of the fees you've paid to this point, and you may endanger your visa status if you leave now," Barnes concluded in a hopeful tone.

"OK, Professor, I'll think about what you said." Kenzo left the office feeling exuberant about his future and without the slightest intent of considering what Barnes had said.

SCENE TEN: EXIT

His final day at Christ Church started as most others had over the past month or so. He awoke in the late morning, well after his first class was underway. He made some Japanese tea that his parents had sent to him in a care package, which had also contained a little note inside that loosely translated said, "Son, we are very proud of you and think of you all of the time. Please remember that we love you and know that you will always bring honor to the family." He knew he did not have the strength to speak with them before he left Oxford, so he'd decided that he would contact them about his plan after his journey had begun. He was convinced that his father would disown him. His mother would be traumatized but would forgive him in time.

He packed up the few things he would be taking with him and waited for his roommate to return. Douglas had been a good friend to Kenzo and had tried desperately to prevent him from leaving Oxford. When Douglas returned from his morning class Kenzo was waiting for him.

"Right man, you're really going through with this. I thought you'd change your mind once you had one final night to sleep on it." Douglas looked concerned. He placed his bag on his desk and sat down next to Kenzo.

"No, I feel more certain than I did last night. I know it's the right thing for me to do." Kenzo smiled as he spoke, hoping to put Douglas at ease.

"You know your father will absolutely blow his top. People are dangerous when they become desperate—especially when their pride is involved."

Kenzo knew he was right but had to pretend otherwise. "He will be very upset at first, but he'll relax once I tell him that I'm just taking a short break and will return to school next semester."

"But that's rubbish," Douglas said. "You told me yourself that you have no interest in returning to school."

"That may be true, but I don't need to tell him that, at least not straight away." Kenzo wanted to change the subject because their conversation was making him depressed. "You can have the things that I left in the room. I gave most of my clothes away to the animal rescue charity shop."

"That's mad," Douglas protested. "I'm not taking all of your things. First off, I don't want this stuff and second, it must be worth five thousand quid. Kenzo, your fucking computer, come on! You said you'd just leave me with bits and bobs, not everything you own."

"Don't worry," Kenzo said reassuringly. "You don't even need to keep it. I'll come back at the end of the school year to pick it up."

Douglas stared at him with a grin on his face. "That's rubbish too. You'll probably be in Finland by the time the year ends. If that happens, I swear I'll sell it all and give the money to charity."

Kenzo stood to go. "Do whatever you would like. I really don't care. You've been a great roommate. I'll send you updates as I go along." Kenzo smiled at his friend, and they hugged.

As Kenzo headed down the old hallway to get his bike he remembered one last thing. He turned back towards their room. Douglas was standing in the doorway, having been watching him go.

Kenzo asked politely, "Could you return my key to the housing office for me?

I'm a little hesitant to do it myself."

Douglas was now grinning widely. "OK Kenzo I will. Make sure your helmet doesn't fully cover your hair. It will help the cars see you in the dark."

They both laughed as Kenzo handed him the keys, waved his last goodbye, and headed back down the hallway.

On his way out of Christ Church he rode his bike through the center of the quad. He knew he was not supposed to ride through there, but he wanted to get one last look at the beautiful buildings as he left. His front basket had a little bag with some snacks. He'd filled his small backpack with a change of clothes, a raincoat and the money he'd taken from the bank account his parents had set up for him. As he pedaled slowly through the quad, one of the guards began flapping their arms at him and a few of the Harry Potter tourists took Kenzo's picture. He waved as he went by.

Once he exited the college, he noted that the streets of Oxford were packed as usual. Tourists jostled with the locals for walking room on the sidewalks. Kenzo turned his bike onto the main street heading out of town. He was tired of living in such a precious, cherished place. He was certain that people deeply loving Oxford had the effect of taking away part of its soul.

After a short while he passed the city limits and cycled onto a pretty English lane bordered by tall hedges on either side. He did not feel as though he was becoming a free man. He felt more alive than free, although, he supposed, these feelings were related. He'd always told himself that he appreciated biking more than most people because he'd not been allowed to ride much as a child. He loved the smell and feel of the air as he rode. He enjoyed the way his long hair blew back from his face. His mind drifted into a quiet state as he pushed the pedals.

He was on his way.

SECTION TWO:
POEMS

CATBIRD

Oh, you're like a catbird lolling
around in bed in your underwear
on this late summer morning
just reading some poems
not cleaning
not yardworking
not working for unpaid hours

Stealing time I suppose
family hustling a floor below
getting ready to leave,
we have to go

"Papa, you ready?"

"Yup." I lied.

CORONA FOURTH

The dog doesn't care much for the Fourth of July
I can't say I blame her or disagree
All these explosions to celebrate
What America?
False Promises?
The bitter strife you've sown?

And of the dispossessed, the disassociated, the dis-ease,
the drugged-up Whites and incarcerated Blacks?
What are you blowing up about?
Oh yes, the masquerade, the lies,
hidden in plain view.

For Pooja

LET IT BE KNOWN

Let it be known that she was loved by us.

May we come in abundance
to weep, to shine
to honor that commitment
to her, to each other
to let the family in through the door of our affection.

So that we may, in some small measure,
help heal the wound of absence.

ANNIVERSARY

On a day near the anniversary of your death
I eat my noodle soup
and look out this window
dreaming onto the town and passersby

    Here we used to be together

Now that you're gone, I am mostly invisible
staring lonely,
wondering what the walking people are talking about
how they are living

You knew everyone
you greeted them through this same glass
and radiated joy

The main thing is
I miss you

Lovely you
and the warmth of the soup,
gone too soon

SECTION THREE:
A CLEANSING

I.

The dreams made his sleep uneasy. Age made his sleep uneasy too, but the dreams were the cause of his nighttime difficulties. In the dreams, he was not sure where the stories began or ended, and he often woke confused and with a leaking, full bladder. As he dreamt, the one thing he knew for sure was that he had done something terribly wrong, was about to be discovered, so had to flee. But he could not find his way through the darkness.

During his waking hours, the bad feelings left. He was grateful for his little bed, the small window in his room and the ritual of wretched food brought in three times a day. He was grateful for his hour outside and for the kindness shown to an old man by the guards who liked him. But when he drifted off to sleep, the fear would return. As he faded out of consciousness, he always knew they were coming for him, and he knew he deserved it. In his waking hours there would be no more daydreams about afternoon romps with his mistress. No fond memories of early evening frolics in the yard with his children. Just doom. His mind betrayed him.

When he was ordering the rapes and disappearances and torture, he was able to neatly compartmentalize his actions. As he grew older, he became less facile and less able to wall off his miserable traits from his admirable ones. His mind was merging into what it was in the beginning: a small organic computer, forwarding sensory information, blending feelings into one indistinct whole.

But that was not the entire truth. Sometimes, in the later part of the night when he was deep asleep, he would wake up crying or screaming. These were not tears for the sorrow of humanity, but for the terror he had personally activated in the world. He would wake suddenly, heart pounding, body sweating, with the echoes of tortured souls screaming profane, unspeakable things, driving him out of sleep, beckoning him to come.

II.

His earliest memories were of music. His mother was born in Italy and sang little songs poorly in Italian until her voice faded with age. When he was young, the songs sounded warm and beautiful. She rarely sang to him or to anyone, but their house was small, so he could hear her in the next room or through his bedroom window as she hung the wash. It made him feel comfortable and loved. He thought Italian was musical as a spoken language and even more musical in song.

He was a reclusive child. He played with his older brothers, but stayed mostly to himself until school-aged, and even then, spent much of his time alone. He imagined his lack of interaction with people as a young child had more to do with his love of the natural world than his isolation from it. He would wander for hours in the parks near his home. He would often bring a bucket with him and scoop up as many ants as possible, and then bring them to another ant colony to do battle. He loved watching the confusion and fear of all those fighting, lost insects.

III.

The irritated guard had come to his cell with breakfast: a small bit of eggs with beef and bread. There would be no coffee today. This guard did not like him. The general was terrified of this one. He feared most of the new guards. He always suspected they were agents sent in to kill him. So many people hated him and on such a deep level: most of the country's left wing, trade unionists, the educated working class, some of the middle class and a good portion of the country's working mothers. The radical leftists worried him the most. The general reasoned they were not afraid to embrace violence as a political tool. If they could get to him in the prison, they would kill him. He was sure the only reason he had not been assassinated yet was that many of the prison guards came from military or police backgrounds and looked back fondly on the junta.

Once the guard left his cell, the general smelled his food to detect any strange odors and inspected it closely for odd colors. Every time this guard brought in his food, he looked at the old general with a knowing smirk. On more than one occasion he had skipped meals, as he was certain he saw spit in the food. The general's sight and smell were both failing him, but checking his food was an old habit. On this occasion the food seemed fine, so he prayed to Jesus, gave thanks and ate.

IV.

He was a frail boy who could never match his peers physically. He learned how to influence people in other ways. When he began to play with the neighbors, they would often band themselves together against other groups of boys. When fights were about to start or retribution needed to be meted out, he was usually the one who did the organizing — he rarely fought. On occasion, they would corner one or two boys and he would decide their punishment. He was never captured himself. If he sensed any danger, he always had an escape route planned. As a child he knew this was cowardice, but as he grew into adulthood, he began to view his timidity as a well-honed survival skill that others lacked. From a young age, whenever danger approached, he would feel a peculiar, sexual charge in his groin. He knew many of the boys were stronger and foolishly braver, which meant that physical hostilities were best left to other people. He was generally quick enough with his tongue to explain away his behavior to his accomplices.

One of his only fights occurred when he was about ten years old. A crowd gathered around him and another boy as they argued about a bicycle. The other boy was a year older, but they were similar in size. Once they started punching each other, he began to panic. His intense sobbing, combined with the physical exertion of fighting, left him gasping for air. After a few moments he surrendered and fell to the ground. This incited the other boy to jump on top of him and begin pounding his head and body. His crying was heard by a mother in a nearby house, who chased off all the boys. His friends later teased him, saying that he sounded like a dying, stuck pig.

V.

When the general had his hour in the prison yard, he would often lie down in the dirt to let the rays of the sun warm his face. The younger prisoners in the adjoining yards found this amusing and would yell at him.

He was well known in the prison. Some of the prisoners who liked him would yell as he lay there, "General, if we could, we'd help you up."

Prisoners who hated him would yell horrible things, "I hope you never get up you bastard," or, "I wish the mothers were here to stomp on your head," or, "To heap stones on the pig. That would be justice."

He mostly ignored the comments, protected as he was by his personal fence. Lying in the yard like this reminded him of spending summer days in Buenos Aires' parks with his family. He loved the smell and feel of the earth beneath his body. His being was a powerful intermediary between the relentlessness of gravity and the center of the earth.

On this day he chose to enjoy the beautiful spring weather by relaxing on the ground. Alonso, the new, irritable guard, was watching him. Although the general had lost some of his intuition in the last few years, this guard made him nervous. Alonso barely spoke to him but joked with the other guards. After being on the ground for some time, the general often had a difficult time getting to his feet. His arthritic joints had stolen what remained of his youth. When other guards were with him in the box they would often step in and help him up. Alonso stood and stared.

"Alonso, could you help me up please? My knees don't work like they used to," he said in a submissive tone.

Alonso waited for several seconds before responding impassively, "You made it down there, which means you can make it back up."

The general had to crawl over then grab at the chain link fence to pull himself up. It took him a long time to get to his feet.

VI.

From a young age he wanted to be a military man. His father was a low-level officer in the Argentine military. He could not disassociate his father's smell from the wool of his father's military uniform. His father would don his dress uniform whenever there were special ceremonies to attend or local events to preside over. The general loved that uniform and the way his father looked in it. It represented things his father represented: security, order, control. Although his parents had reservations about sending him to cadet school—his father wanted him to be a doctor or lawyer and his mother did not want him to move out of their home at all—he begged them both so determinedly that they stopped trying to prevent him. He conspired to make them agree. He told his father that he could practice law or medicine in the military (even though he had no plans to do so). He promised his mother that he would come home for every break and holiday, and argued that the Argentinian military produced polite, well-organized, hardworking boys. He left for cadet school in the fall of his fourteenth year.

During his first year at the Academia Militar de Buenos Aires, much to his mother's chagrin, he only went home occasionally on holidays, even though the school was less than twenty miles from his house. The hazing at the school was severe for first-year cadets. He did not shy away from it. He knew that if he pretended to be fearless, the older cadets would do him favors, which would help him rise through the social ranks more quickly. The general's attitude during the hazing period did earn him a reputation for bravery. Once he became an upperclassman, he quickly rose to a leadership position at the school. People listened and acted when he spoke. He learned to cultivate and use this power to his advantage.

VII.

Today was bathing day. Twice during the week, he was marched out of his cellblock into the main part of the prison to take a shower. He was kept separate from the regular prison population for his own safety. Normally he loved this day. It was an opportunity, even with its inherent dangers, to stretch his tired legs and expand his small world. However, he had begun to calculate, based on the guard rotation, when Alonso would be working. He realized, with a dull dread, that Alonso would escort him today. He had been unsettled by Alonso's presence well before the incident in the yard, but it was further confirmation Alonso was on someone's payroll and the general was the target. Bathing day was a time he was most vulnerable to attack. The shower room was in the basement at the end of a long, windowless, putrid-smelling corridor. The room itself was small for such a large prison. There were no places to sit down, and each wall had ten showerheads squeezed together. The room had been entirely tiled at some point but was badly in need of repair. Broken tiles and bits of grout lay about the floor. It was an especially treacherous place for old men, as there was nothing to hang on to.

His heartbeat quickened as the footsteps of the guard approached his cell. He gripped his towel and soap with clenched fists and weakening knees. When he saw the guard's head through the door's small upper opening, he let out an unplanned sigh of relief. It was not Alonso after all; he must have confused the days, or they switched the guard rotation. Either way, it was a blessing.

VIII.

Argentina's real wars were internal. The stage play for the country and for most of Latin America was set as soon as the conquering Spaniards and Portuguese landed on the southern continent. Once the European planters beat back enough native people and enslaved enough Africans, it had been a long fight between the forces of elite reaction and the resisting lower classes. When he joined the army it meant taking a side, that he was a member of an organization dedicated to the survival of the owning class. He would not have been able to articulate this position as a young man, but he knew where his father stood in the conflict.

As he aged into adulthood, he developed an unquenchable desire for prestige and a blinding faith in the sanctity of the state and the Catholic Church. When he joined the army following cadet school he knew, with conviction, that he would serve as a force for good and order in his country.

One of his first missions as a young officer involved going to a rural town to help "pacify" the population. The leader of the military expedition was a lieutenant colonel named De La Torre. From the start it was clear not only that the lieutenant colonel had no moral or ethical sensibilities, but that he may have been insane. In his army experience the general met only a few people who he thought were truly disturbed. De La Torre was one.

The town they were pacifying had a technical university that fostered leftist organizing against the regime. There had been a series of recent attacks on government buildings. Students and trade unionists were the suspected culprits. Many of the undergraduates in the town had joined the local bus drivers in their protest for higher wages. De La Torre's technique for dealing with this problem was to have his soldiers attend student gatherings in plainclothes, befriend any leaders or likely leaders, and then report their names.

One day in late summer De La Torre sent him to a rural house where the army interrogated these potential enemies of the state. The house was at the end of a long drive, but he could hear the screaming before he was halfway down the driveway. Two bored-looking soldiers, insensible to the noises, guarded the front door. As he entered the house, the screaming became intermittent, but was coupled with a terrible sickening smell. He felt his knees start to give. A soldier at the top of the cellar stairs pointed down, and so he went. The screaming had become convulsive sobbing.

The cellar had low ceilings, a dirt floor and was very poorly lit at the landing. To his right he could see what looked like an old barn door propped slightly open with a well-illuminated room beyond. The stench on this level was an overpowering mixture of sewage and some other acrid odor he could not identify. He pushed open the door and had to catch his breath. A group of five enlisted men were standing around a wooden animal pen, looking down on a young man who was naked and hog-tied on the floor. His face was beaten to a swollen pulp, and he was struggling through a pile of his own excrement to move away from the soldiers. When the men saw him enter the room they immediately stood at attention and saluted. After returning their salutes and nodding his approval, he turned around and walked back up the stairs. Once he left the house he walked calmly into the backyard. When he found a hidden spot behind some bushes he bent over and vomited. He then gathered himself, returned to the house and conducted his first of many interrogations.

IX.

He woke sobbing with children's cries still ringing in his ears and a wet spot on his bed. His heart was beating so fast he thought he might be dying. He dreamt he was running out the front door of his childhood home to find the source of a high-pitched noise at dusk. He ran, unclothed, towards the sound. He stumbled through thickets that were higher than his head. As he got closer, he became sure it was a child or children in distress. He looked down to see that his arms were covered in blood from scratches. The sun was setting, but there was still some light filtering through the leafed-out branches. In the distance he could see the woods were thinning out into a wide opening. He could hear animal sounds mixed in with children's cries. In the clearing he came upon a pack of dogs dismembering a small boy, who squealed as they pulled away his flesh. A smaller pack of dogs circled a second boy, who was attempting to crawl away. The first child was badly disfigured. Neither had any hope of escaping.

He tried desperately to run away but the whole spectacle was so sickeningly mesmerizing, he was momentarily frozen, unable to react. As he returned to his senses he fled, crashing through the brambles running towards home with the children's screams and the encroaching dark close on his heels.

The general banged the cell door with his cup to attract the attention of a guard. He needed to wash the urine off his body. His fear of rousing the wrong guard was outweighed by his pride; he refused to sit in his own waste. He put his ear to the door and listened—nothing. He started to bang again but before he could really begin making further racket, he saw Alonso glaring at him through the hole in the door.

"What do you want old man?" Alonso always used the "tu" form, which the general found offensive and rude.

The look in the guard's eyes made the general begin to rethink his desire to wash his clothes, but he pressed on with something of his old sense of dignity. "I would like to go to the bathroom to wash up," the general stated meekly, somewhere between a question and a request.

"It would be an honor to help you, but unfortunately I have a hundred other prisoners to look after. So why don't you stop banging your cup on the door and go fuck yourself."

He hung his wet clothes on the end of his cot and spent the rest of the night naked, curled up on his bed shivering under his light blanket.

X.

The time the general spent at the height of his power was deeply fulfilling. The press had not predicted he would be selected to lead the junta. Even some of his best friends in the military elite were surprised by his ascension. But by then, he had shown his loyalty to the ruling establishment. For almost twenty years he was an unquestioning servant, dutifully fulfilling his mandate to help create order in a disordered state. At the time he was named as the country's leader, he had been military intelligence chief for several years. This meant there were very few acts of political repression he had not authorized or personally overseen. These activities ranged from spying on dissidents and radicals to torture and extrajudicial executions. He worked unwaveringly to undermine the power of the socialist threat to the country. He personally managed attacks on and torture of leftist rebels who were operating from the mountains and in the cities' poorer neighborhoods. His superiors noticed his uncommon passion for such missions. He developed intimate contacts with Argentina's judges, corporate and political leaders and US operatives. These connections provided him a luxurious car with a personal driver, an attractive mistress in the suburbs, a large home for his family in a different suburb and a generous expense account to supplement his salary. His three children attended private schools, and his wife was the hub of the officers' social gatherings. By the time he was announced as president (following a coup d'état), he controlled large sections of Argentina's military-industrial network.

To reward people who buoyed his climb, as president he stepped up attacks on dissidents with more aggressive tactics. He began to order, with guidance from the junta's networks, disappearances of the state's real and perceived enemies. This internal housekeeping helped to solidify his grip on power. Within the first year of his presidency, his career-long efforts had finally come to fruition for him and his family. One of the few interruptions to his serenity was the sound of protestors (mostly mothers of people disappeared by the government) in the plaza near the presidential mansion. He would sometimes hear them calling his name and banging on pots as he drifted off to sleep.

XI.

Today his son was coming to visit him in prison. The general thought his emotional response to seeing his family would dull with time, but the reverse seemed to be happening. When he thought about his family or wrote them letters, he would often weep. They were tears of nostalgia and loss. His wife had died five years before of breast cancer, just as the government was moving to revoke the pardon that had ended his previous sentence for war crimes. Lonely in prison, he acutely regretted the lack of time he spent with her as she was dying. His obsession with his own well-being seemed reasonable, given the severity of the resurrected charges against him. But now, especially since there was never really any chance of him avoiding reconviction, he began to see he had abandoned her.

Of their three children only one still lived in Argentina. His oldest son had moved to the US, and his daughter to Spain—ostensibly to escape the broken Argentinian economy, but they faced intense social pressure simply by sharing his last name. The country had turned fully against the former junta and its operatives. Paco, his youngest child, lived with his wife and two children in a middle-class suburb outside of Buenos Aires. He was a stable and emotionally distant child.

He intended to tell Paco about his fears concerning the guard. There had been other instances during his imprisonment when Paco needed to calm him down. When the general thought about it objectively, a story about a rogue guard who was out to get him sounded a bit implausible. Although, he was sure if he gave Paco the details, his son would be able to get the guard moved out of his section. He thought Paco could be swayed on account of previous instances of retribution against imprisoned junta members.

As Paco approached, he noticed his son looked tired and drawn. After exchanging kisses, the general expressed his concern.

"Paco are you OK? You look very tired."

"I'm alright Papa. Don't worry about me."

After chatting about the family, he decided to get his son's attention by relaying the incident of the dream and his wet clothing. After the general described the details of that night, his son just looked distractedly out of one of the high windows in the visiting room. The general decided to take a different approach.

He grabbed his son's hands. "I'm frightened of this guard Paco. I'm sure he's an agent sent to kill me."

Paco looked exasperated. "Papa, please. Don't you realize all the guards are underpaid and overworked? He is just a person doing a stressful job for very little pay. Please don't let this happen again. You get so worked up about your opinions, but really, it will be OK."

He was getting desperate. "No Paco you don't understand. This is different. I can see the hatred in his eyes and hear it in his voice."

"Yes, many of the guards know who you are and probably don't like you, but that doesn't mean they want to kill you. You also know many other guards hold the junta in high esteem. This guard would not risk his job to kill an elderly man who is living out his life in prison."

"Paco, please just speak with the warden. Just a few words to let him know what's happening."

Paco stood up to leave. "No Papa. Even if there was an issue here, which there is not, I have no influence in this place. My speaking with the warden could make your life worse. I'm certain he is not one of your supporters. Just try to stay relaxed and not worry so much. That's what you must do. I have to go home because Marin is working the late shift this week."

As Paco hugged and kissed him goodbye, he was sure this was the end. His son was his only hope and now that was gone. Later that night as he drifted off to sleep, he imagined himself as a stranded, dying rabbit in a wide-open field, listening intently to the beating wings of an approaching hawk.

XII.

It was startling how fast his friends and colleagues deserted him once the junta fell from power. During his first trial, he steadfastly maintained his innocence and claimed to be ignorant of the charges brought by the new, elected government. Ultimately, they called an enormous number of witnesses to testify against him, many of whom provided very detailed, graphic evidence of his culpability. The prosecution's case went on for so long he sometimes fell asleep during the testimony, which prompted some members of the press to label him cold-blooded. Once he was convicted, the only people who vouched for his character during sentencing were his immediate family members. Most of the other junta leaders, who could have testified on his behalf, had feared for their skins, and had fled the country or gone into hiding.

His first round of imprisonment went as well as he could have hoped. Because the government wanted to make sure he did not become a martyr for the right, he was kept in a well-maintained cell away from the general prison population. After five years he was released, when the new government decided that it would implement a "peace and rec- onciliation" program. They let most of the former junta members free, under the agreement the junta leaders would testify at truth hearings.

When he left the prison there was a small group of supporters to greet him. There was also a very vocal group of people who were not pleased with the government's ideas about reconciliation and screamed insults as he was driven away. During the truth hearings (on the advice of his lawyers) he admitted to a few of the atrocities the regime committed. He provided some information about the junta's actions, but he did not reveal much beyond events that were publicly known. His lawyer suspected there might come a time when a change in government could lead to a change in thinking about his presiden- cy, and any testimony he gave could later be used against him.

Within four years of gaining his freedom the government did change, and the new regime decided that certain crimes were too significant to be pardoned and that the pardons issued to members of the junta—his being highest on the list—were invalid and unjust. There were untold numbers of people that would not rest until the government put him and the other leaders back in jail. His enemies got their wish. Not only was his pardon revoked, but new, more severe charges were filed, and his truth commission testimony was used against him. When the judges at his second trial shared their verdict with the court—guilty on all counts—it was the final confirmation the process had been a mere formality.

During this sentencing hearing, there were no people to testify on his behalf. His wife was too sick to leave her bed. His children, while still professing their love in private, wanted nothing to do with the trial, which had become a public spectacle. When the judges announced he would be spending the rest of his life in prison, he was able to keep his composure. As he was whisked from the courthouse to the prison van, there were no supporters this time. There were, however, a large group of reporters pressing microphones to his face and an even larger group of people rallying against him. Some protesters spat and threw things at him, while others cried tears of joy about him being permanently removed from society.

XIII.

The general never thought deeply about what the last day of his life would be like, although he'd assumed it would be full of the mundane tasks and activities that order most lives. He worried about death almost every day, but he knew this was due mainly to his cowardice. He could not really grasp the idea of dying, other than to be afraid.

The past few weeks had been difficult. His dreams were as terrible as ever, and his waking life had become more of a struggle. Alonso was now openly malevolent towards him. Back in the days when he had power, he could have ordered Alonso's execution for any number of trivial offenses. The general would have ensured Alonso's family suffered too. He had asked a couple of the more sympathetic guards if they could get him an appointment with the warden. They told him the chance of arranging such a meeting was highly unlikely.

The general developed a nasty little flu that made him feel especially weak and tired. When he woke up, he felt horribly cold, even though it was midsummer. Today was bathing day. He was dreading it. His shower time was not until late afternoon, and he already felt sick to his stomach.

As he waited for the hour to come, he concocted a plan. He would lie in bed and refuse his breakfast and lunch, with the idea being to impress upon the early shift guards how sick he was. By the time Alonso came to take him to the shower it would be clear he was too sick to move. The problem with the plan was that it was almost true; he had no appetite and very little energy. He refused breakfast and then lunch. Neither of the first two guards seemed interested in his condition or lack of hunger.

He spent much of the day sweating and shivering under his blanket. His mind rolled around to different scenes of his life in a feverish jumble. He could not settle on one person or concentrate on one train of thought for long: his children playing in the yard when they were young, the beauty of his wife on their wedding day, his first day in power as president, his feelings of terror on entering prison. He tried to pray, hoping the prayers would stop the unsteadiness of his mind.

It was early evening when the footsteps approached his door. There was a loud clang as the old lock opened.

When Alonso entered the cell in his white prison guard uniform, the general was not immediately certain who the guard was. "Get up," Alonso said calmly. "It's shower time."

The general sat up in his bed. "I can't go today—I'm sick. I've eaten nothing all day. I need to stay here to rest," his voice cracked.

Alonso approached the bed and stood over him; he was a young man, perhaps in his early 30s, of average height, with dark hair, large hands, and broad shoulders. The general was petrified.

The guard whispered threateningly through gritted teeth, "You're an old man and you are sick. You need to bathe." Alonso grabbed the general roughly under both arms and lifted him out of bed.

The general began to sob. He stammered weakly, "I need my things."

"No, you don't," Alonso said as he grabbed him tightly by one arm and wrapped his other arm around the general's bony shoulders.

They stumbled as they walked. The general wept quietly and tried to drag his feet, but it was no use. Just before they reached the long corridor that led to the shower room the general tried to break off and flee towards the nearest cellblock. Alonso caught him after two steps. He squeezed the general so hard his bladder let go.

The hallway to the bathing room summoned them. They walked into it: twenty meters, ten meters, the strong smell of rotten water. They were close now. As they entered the chamber, he felt Alonso's powerful hands on his back pushing him forcefully towards the tiled wall. As his body flew through the air, he was not sure if they were the hands of God or the hands of the devil, but he knew, with absolute clarity, he would die on this day.

SECTION FOUR:
POEMS

BEECHES

The beech trees are stubborn,
they insist, against the coming elements,
that summer is still here.

How can I deny them, why should I?
We are both entwined with our temporal existence,
but they are unfettered, undeterred and unruffled.

I am fettered, deterred, and ruffled.
Maybe if I watch close
I can see another way.

PERIHELION

Living, dying, juxtaposed on the last day of your life
in an antiseptic hospital room with a mercifully west-facing window
and a perch wide enough for me to lay in and sun for you to boot

We were both cats dozing as light erupted from the January afternoon sun,
a mere 91,000,000 miles away
Sunbathing was always a great joy of yours, I imagine it still is
although you are now here and not, which,
apart from our grand delusion,
is the case for all of us I suppose

When I am quiet, the only thing to hear,
between your long-separated deep breathing,
is the tick of the morphine-machine
I fell asleep for a moment and forgot where I was, where are you?

What if I rolled you out of this room by the staff
to the elevator and out the door?
I don't have an ambulance, so I'd have to wheel you down the road
(hopefully the drivers will turn a blind eye, it is Florida after all)

CONTINUED...

to the beach, just a few miles away,
nothing like 91,000,0000

I would disrobe you and put you gently down in the sand
(hoping for more blind eyes from beachgoers)
You would have to wait as I constructed your vessel
The breakers here are small
After strapping you in I would swim out with you as far as I can
— you are too weak to paddle yourself —
and give you one last push

The final worry, of course, are the boats close to shore,
those further out would probably think what they saw was an apparition,
which is what we both must hope for

WEEP

Adult children may ask themselves this question as they watch their parents die,
"What if I don't weep?"

I needn't have worried.
I spewed forth like a bleeding hyena.
I choked on my breath.
I stood shell-shocked.
I mumbled to myself.
I cried like a baby without a mother,
like a creature without a lover in this world.

ROOFS

Roofs have protected us over these many years, decades really
you from a tiny nugget til now
Butchered with storms,
hovering between us and the howling winds of blizzards
dropping their accumulated weight,
soft, delicate, soundless

We were dreaming, living in sickness and health,
minds and bodies contending with our own
and the earth's unyieldingness

You will leave here and head into the tumbled masses
of the insane, the ill-reputed and the saints
Show kindness and charity to all
Fight through the folly and help mold us to better favor,
the owls and we will hoot and holler upon your return

SECTION FIVE:
ZOMBIES IN HILLINGDON

Here we stand or here we fall
History won't care at all
Make the bed, light the light
Lady mercy won't be home tonight

Yeah, you don't waste no time at all
Don't hear the bell but you answer the call
It comes to you as to us all
Hey, we're just waiting
For the hammer to fall

– QUEEN

"Goddamn this fucking mower!" I had many moments like this, worried about trifles, before the "zombies" came to London. I'd left the suburbs of Cleveland looking for any sign I was still a living animal. I'm not sure if there is a more uninteresting, soul-sucking place on earth than suburban Cleveland. What can prepare a person for nonexistence in Ohio? Miles of cul-de-sac homes interspersed with strip malls, interesting only if you tried to distinguish them from each other. After spending years living like this and wondering if I might as well dig myself a grave in the backyard, my manager offered me a job in our London plant. I worked as a middle manager at an American box company. The upper management team wanted to make our small factory outside of London a bigger factory. They thought exporting a bunch of American managers would speed up the process. Bullshit, of course, but at least I got out.

I ended up living in a small town in the west London suburbs that was almost as ridiculous as what I'd left. The local government council prided itself on having the most "green spaces" of any London borough, but my new neighborhood was wall-to-wall brick sameness. Maybe they had to promote the parks to prevent people from going completely mad. Most homes were duplexes built after the Second World War to accommodate the baby boom. I'd accepted the job to escape my tedious, pathetic life in Middle America, only to be relocated to a new, equally tedious and pathetic life. I guess it's good to be careful what you wish for.

Even with the unfortunate similarities, I enjoyed myself more than I had during my last years in America; at least I wasn't in Cleveland. I went to the local pub to watch soccer, befriended some of my neighbors, made a regular slog into London on the tube to visit the free, crowded museums and gawk at the wealth on display. Before the collapse, there was more money per square foot in the center of London than anywhere else on earth. I'm sure it's still there for those bold enough to seek it out, but the paper money is not worth anything anymore, only the shiny metal.

Although the street I lived on in Hillingdon was dreary to look at and incredibly sleepy, it was the most racially and ethnically diverse place I'd ever lived. The Brits' hubris in the preceding centuries meant diversity in the twenty-first. There were people from all over the former empire living on my street. From Pakistanis to Nigerians, they'd all decided to pay a visit to the mothership and then decided it was better to live in the former master's backyard than in his outhouse.

My neighbors, Ian and Sadie, who shared the other side of my "semi-detached" house (a British duplex) were a lovely, retired couple from Scotland and Ireland respectively. We shared chats in our connected front driveways about their kids and grandkids, who were spread out over Greater London. They would send me postcards when they went traveling, with short notes about the weather, or the drive, or tidbits about some landmark they had seen. I began to return the favor when I took trips around Europe. They would bring me treats from their grandkids' birthday parties and I would bring them things from my travels. Ian had been in the British Merchant Marine and loved talking with me about where he'd been in the US. They both liked me, although our relationship never evolved beyond being pleasant neighbors. They escaped Hillingdon before the real terror started, but I have no idea if they are alive or dead. Their only hope was their children. Older people did not last very long against the storm.

At first, like many big moments in life, the changes were rumors. There had been a sighting in Belarus of a stark-naked man devouring a pigeon in the middle of a city park on a late summer evening. It got picked up on one of the many internet news feeds, filed under the subheading of "Crazy Shit You Hear About in the Former Soviet Union." This man got to work ripping off the bird's beak with his mouth as it struggled to get out of his grip, and then plucked the bird feather by feather as mothers strolling with children screamed bloody murder. Because there had been no video footage of the event, and because the man in question was never found, the story died. Unfortunately for humanity, the story behind that story really didn't die—it just gestated. With the endless stream of celebrity and atrocity news coursing through the world's cables, the pigeon-bitten-by-man story was filed away in the place reserved for news bloopers and fail vlogs. Of course, given what's happened, I could use a few light-hearted blooper videos.

The second, more significant incident took place closer to England, and was much harder to ignore—impossible, actually—because it happened on live television. Belgium, it turns out, was like most other countries in that much of its television programming had morphed into absurd "reality" farces and "celebrity" quiz shows. The program, "The Evening Scramble," became the most watched television event in human history. The concept of the show was simple enough; Belgian and Dutch "celebrity" hotties were paired with large-brained college professors, who competed against each other at solving complex word puzzles. There was a catch to the show: the losing team had to engage in inane behavior, like removing their clothes and running across the stage.

On the evening in question the noteworthy team consisted of a college professor from Holland and a woman whose only claim to fame was an appearance on a different Belgian reality TV program. The show began innocuously enough, but five minutes into the proceedings it became clear something was about to go seriously wrong.

The audience claps, then the host begins with a big shit-eating grin on his face. "Good evening ladies and gentlemen I'm Dieter Gross and welcome to another edition of 'The Evening Scramble.'"

"Tonight," he continues, "we've got a lovely show for you. Our two teams are very evenly matched with some serious brain and beauty combinations and a wicked end for the losers that you will have to see to believe." Someone on stage makes a funny, gagging noise, but it's hard to tell who it is and Dieter does not seem to notice. "Behind the blue podium we have Professor of Asian Studies Willem Drimble from Utrecht teamed with the gorgeous Anna Malinta from Belgium's 'Big Brother.' Wave to the audience team blue."
Gross points towards the blue podium, with the camera following his gesture, but neither Blue Team member is smiling or waving. The blond woman with fake breasts, faker hair, and piles of makeup stares at Drimble and does her best to lean as far away from him as possible. Drimble does the opposite. He leans towards his partner with a very disturbing, nasty look on his face. He appears dishevelled and slightly disoriented. His clothing hangs loosely off his body, as if it were made for someone two sizes larger than him. His eyes are droopy and bloodshot. Although the camera stays on them for only a moment, something is noticeably wrong with the professor. (Because the video went viral so quickly, essentially becoming the most important piece of television footage ever broadcast, people watched it enough times so that details that might have been missed with one or two viewings became obvious after the tenth.)

When the camera pans back to Dieter, he has lost some of his forced enthusiasm. While the camera stays on him, he keeps looking towards Anna and

Willem. After a moment he realizes he's lost the thread. His smile returns and he begins to introduce the Blue Team's opponents, but when the camera pans to the Red Team they are not looking at Dieter. They're looking at the Blue Team with very concerned expressions on their faces.

Dieter hesitates for another moment and then begins to introduce the Red Team. "OK, from the prestigious…" That's as far as he gets. There is a mumbled, crunching noise in the background followed by bloodcurdling screams from both Red Team contestants, their eyes locked on the Blue Team. The camera lingers for a moment on the Red Team, then it pans back to the Blue Team, which makes it very evident why the Red Team members were shrieking. Professor Drimble has his partner's blond hair firmly gripped between his two hands and has blood all over his face.

The video cuts out right at that point, and while it was hard to tell exactly what happened to Ms. Malinta, it was obvious there was something very wrong with her face.

Once the news programmers and social media sites got word of this incident, it quickly became linked with a bunch of other human-biting-human stories. They had been developing in the pop culture background but were not previously linked with each other. Meanwhile, the frisky professor was finally subdued onstage and put in jail for his actions, although not before he'd bitten half a dozen more people in the process. By the time the medical professionals figured out it was some sort of strange virus, it was too late. The local police force had been infected, along with doctors, nurses, and the entire television station crew.

The UK closed its coastline and borders almost overnight. It was, in the end, a testimony to what many of the government's critics had been saying all along: Great Britain, in the early part of the twenty-first century, was just a security state masquerading as a democracy. All the trumped-up justifications used by officials to explain the UK's enormous security expenditures—ostensibly to defend the country against some unknowable, malevolent force—were now coming from an actual threat. Flights in and out of the country were stopped. The ferries were halted, as was all trade with continental Europe. All phone and internet communication was openly monitored (although most people assumed this had been occurring for many years). Local government authorities were called upon to set up heavily guarded quarantine buildings, should the virus crop up among their citizenries. Schools were closed. People were immediately required to ration food (the large grocery stores, it was correctly assumed, would run out of food very rapidly if people were allowed to stockpile rations). The government also assumed control of the entire energy sector and stationed armed squads at gas stations.

The authorities decided that some businesses were essential, and these were ordered to continue operating until instructed otherwise. Initially, perhaps due to some bureaucratic fuck up, our box factory was deemed essential, so I continued showing up for work. Of course, once the officials realized that there was nothing to put in the boxes, our factory was shut down. It was around this time the little threads that hold human society together started to unwind.

I think this interim shutdown period only lasted a few weeks, although it may have been longer. (As the days droned on, my sense of time slipped a bit.) Initially the changes were subtle. The television stations began playing only British shows. Before the authorities made this switch, most of the foreign news coverage was focused on the virus and the latest efforts of governments to deal with the "human-to-human" attacks. The foreign media blackout was undoubtedly an effort at panic avoidance.

Now that schools and most businesses were shut, people were out on the streets in Hillingdon en masse for the first time since I'd moved to the UK. I'd always explained Hillingdon to my friends and family back home as a place where you only knew you were surrounded by other living humans on account of the garbage they brought out once a week. Now people were in their small front yards and were talking. Since there was no longer much driving to be done, the children commandeered the streets as their own play areas.

The news and rumors that spread about the zombies were not reassuring. It seemed the infection rate, once a stricken person bit another person, was close to a hundred percent, and there was no short-term possibility of a cure. The only certain cure was death, and the only way to stop the spread of the disease was to kill the carrier. Because the infected humans were fundamentally violent towards members of their own species, it became rapidly apparent that rules around murder had to evolve, and fast. Once the UK officials realized the only way to stop the plague was to kill all infected people, the prohibition on humans murdering each other slowly became outdated.

To prevent people from slaughtering each other, the government sent the local councils "advice on handling citizens affected by the Human Hyper-Violence Virus," which was published in local newspapers. The government mandated that only sanctioned authorities could shoot suspected infectees, that children (perhaps in the hope of an eventual cure) suspected of being infected should be afforded the opportunity of quarantine whenever possible, and that citizens with non-ballistic weapons must be "certain beyond all reasonable doubts" before attempting to "eliminate" a zombie in self-defense. Of course, with the UK gun laws being what they were, very few people had immediate access to guns. This posed an extermination constraint, given that dealing a fatal blow to an infected person at close range could lead to further infections from flying blood and other body fluids.

What were the telltale signs that a person had become infected? What attributes would be identifiable enough for noninfected people to overcome their natural pacifism and kill another human being? Making these decisions was especially hard since the infected people reportedly were sensitive to light and did most of their "attacking and snacking" after hours. There was a smell, some said, of dead fish, others said of rotting meat. But how close would you have to get before you could smell them? Their eyes were bloodshot, slightly yellowish, and milky. This was known positively, based on the pre-lockdown video clips. What if you happened to club someone to death who just had a bad cold? Perhaps the most identifiable trait of the infected subjects, beyond their insatiable desire for human flesh, was their lust for shiny objects and large flashy machines. It may sound like a trait of the average corporate head, but this lust was frenzy on a whole different level. The infected beasts jumped into any large, shiny machine they could find—the flashier the better. This was also known for sure because there were viral videos taken of zombies carjacking and driving around in huge, gleaming SUVs. If things had not taken such an unfortunate path, many of the videos would have been humorous, as the virus seemed to seriously impede the zombies' driving abilities. There was even a twenty-second clip of a private jet crashing into the control tower in Brussels, presumably with a zombie at the controls.

Once people were stuck at home with their families, living on food rations, their paranoia flourished. As the time between the government's missives grew longer, people's thoughts turned to defending their families and their streets at any possible cost. It turns out there were some guns in the UK after all. As street-by-street watch committees were formed, much of the community focus turned to arming the adult population, and how to avoid killing noninfected people. This state of crisis gradually brought guns into the neighborhoods. There was a brisk rural to urban exchange, as friends and relatives who lived in the country "found" spare weapons, many of which had passed through generations. While it was true many of these hunting rifles and shotguns were old and bulky (and lacking sufficient ammunition for what was to come), most were in good shape, as they had been treated as family heirlooms. I came to see them as something akin to religious relics. Like Chinese Christians hiding crosses, the guns had been kept in perfect condition away from the eyes of the state.

For many years I'd wanted to get married and have kids, but now, for the first time in my adult life, I felt lucky to not have a family with me. As the communication lines between the UK and the US were gradually shut down, I began to worry about my family back home. My sister was divorced and lived with her two kids in a run-down suburb outside of Chicago. My parents were older when they'd had us, and my mother had died of cancer ten years back. After my mother died, my father's health steadily deteriorated. By the time I moved to England he was living in an assisted-living home in a different dreadful Chicago suburb, not far from my sister. I missed them both, but my relationship with my family was fraught, primarily on account of my father's alcoholism. They loved me and had not wanted me to leave, but part of what drove me to move was the desire to have some distance from them. I told them (and myself) it would be a short-term assignment, and that I would keep in regular touch with them and my nieces, but once the virus struck, it looked more and more as though my move was a semipermanent condition. During the long hours of solitude, waiting, silence and terror that finally came, thinking about my family made me feel sad and helpless.

In some fundamental way, I was not completely shocked by the unfolding events. Although I was as scared and confused as my neighbors, I'd always had a gut-level feeling that the world humanity created for itself in the twenty-first century was doomed to fail. I suppose the only real surprise was the incredible speed of the unwinding.

Patrick and Dawn lived in the duplex next door, on the side away from Ian and Sadie. Patrick was of West Indian descent and worked as a delivery driver for a food service company. Dawn was a night nurse at a local health clinic. They had twin teenage daughters who were preparing for their A-Level exams (somewhat equivalent to a US high school diploma). Once things started shutting down, Patrick and I began having regular, ominous backyard chats. We'd been friendly before the virus came, talking about soccer or the weather over the garden fence. As we became cooped up in the neighborhood, our relationship deepened. I told him I thought the government authorities would set up quarantine stations away from Hillingdon and that they would begin moving families to these areas. We discussed the fact that the neighborhood, while arming itself, was woefully unprepared for an attack.

Eventually the government shut the highways down to nonofficial traffic and began running power only in the evenings. The water supply was my real concern. I figured if we lost that slice of civilization then people would really start to panic. The television also began to move into shutdown mode around this time. (The authorities had restricted and slowed internet access early on). This was less important to me because the BBC had shifted almost completely to canned, rerun programming interspersed with bullshit news reporting masquerading as genuine information. Although, if they had shown what was really happening, I'm sure it would have been quite unsettling. I tried to envision, for example, what India would be like under the assault of the virus. I'd never been there, but I'd seen enough TV footage and spoken with enough people who had been there to understand that a plague like this would usher in pandemonium at an incalculable level. Fueled by the spread of the zombie virus, India's regular disorder and chaos, at least in my imagining, would be a benign preamble to the trouble that would follow—a hellish darkness with little warning and lots of blood.

Once the highways closed, evenings in Hillingdon took on peculiar new qualities; of particular note was the concentrated lack of sound. The doom machine of constantly droning engine noises (from the mass of highways that bisected Hillingdon from every conceivable angle) had been replaced by an ominous silence. Before the virus arrived, I marvelled that I could wake up to take a leak at any time of the night and always hear machines running and tires on pavement.

Until the point when shit became truly serious, the government had provided a couple of food banks in Hillingdon. Neighborhood associations would then retrieve the food from the banks in trucks to distribute at street level. The amount of food distributed gradually diminished. By the time the government sent the elderly and the young away to rural "protection camps," we were down to crackers, some surplus meat, old apples, and hard cheese. I began to venture out in the evenings to see what I could find in the way of provisions. I wasn't necessarily planning to loot from the closed shops, but I needed to know what the options were if the food completely ran out. I carried with me a large hunting knife that I'd brought from the US, which was illegal in the UK but made it through in my checked baggage. I'd also fashioned a small club from the handle of a garden shovel.

There was speculation that infected people were leaving Central London to look for other victims. There were also thoughts that perhaps the shiny, luxury goods the zombies craved were in short supply. The rumor in Hillingdon was that the authorities had heavily armed and fortified the financial district to protect the banks, the museums, and the crown jewels. All of this was done, so the thinking went, at the expense of the middle and working-class neighborhoods. Of course, if the stories were true, they made sense; the wealthy had a lot shinier stuff and governments are really set up at the bidding of the rich and for their protection.

On my second nighttime foray into the surrounding neighborhoods, I was struck by the amount of wildlife wandering around. I saw families of foxes walking down the middle of the streets, raccoons ambling down sidewalks and deer grazing on people's front lawns. It was as if the animals had just been waiting for people to stop driving cars through their territory. It was becoming clear that while the virus was eating into the human world, furry creatures were thriving in this realigned ecosystem.

For this journey I wanted to scope out the condition of the high street shops closest to my house to see if they were being guarded and to see if they were being looted at night. I also wanted to get a glimpse of the A40, which was the main highway east into the city; I figured if the lunatic zombies really were headed our way, they were most likely to drive down the biggest and most obvious roads.

The stores on the high street were unguarded, but most had been covered with metal doors. I continued walking towards the highway. As I approached the overpass, I thought I heard the distant sound of an engine revving sporadically. I felt a wave of panic and froze in my spot. I stopped breathing and listened more intently. It was indeed an engine noise and seemed to be getting closer. It sounded like the driver was stepping on the gas pedal erratically. The car was definitely heading west, towards Hillingdon. I tried to convince myself that it was just a military truck patrolling the highway. I was still harboring the illusion we would never see infected people in Hillingdon, that the virus was weakening as it passed from human to human. I suppose everyone who knew it was coming must have tried to convince themselves with a similar line of thinking. My curiosity gradually unglued my feet. I walked up the gently sloped overpass, on the east side of the road (so that I could look towards the direction of the engine noise), trying to stay close to the high hedge that bordered the sidewalk.

As I crested the overpass it was clear that the car was close now. I peeked through the bushes and saw the empty, dark highway. Just at the far edge of my vision, a pair of headlights swerved back and forth, heading west on the wrong side of the motorway. When it got to within a quarter of a mile of the bridge, I could tell it was not a car, but an enormous, black SUV. It was coming on at a high rate of speed. I felt sure, based on its pace, it would not try to exit at Hillingdon. The headlights got closer. My stomach churned; my heart jumped in my chest. Just before it would have been too late to take the exit, the driver turned the car sharply to the right, slammed on the gas and climbed up the entry ramp.

I thought I was going to shit myself. I was exposed on the sidewalk with nowhere to hide. Just as I considered hurling my body into the thorny hedgerow there was a loud crash at the top of the ramp. The driver did not manage the turn where the ramp met the access road and crashed directly into a cement roundabout. The front of the SUV buckled badly, the side doors crumpled, and the airbags deployed inside the cabin.

What the fuck was in that car? I was less than a hundred feet away from the crash. In any normal circumstance I would have run to the car to help. I knew if I did it might be the last Good Samaritan act of my life. I stayed crouched and watched. After a minute or two the driver was able to force the door open. It looked to be a man of average build. I could hear him making guttural, muttering sounds as he spilled out of the car. Still, I waited. He turned in my direction and started to stumble towards me. I wasn't sure if he could see me. I had only seconds to make a move. I turned and sprinted towards the high street. At that moment, he saw me and yelled something unintelligible.

Was his voice actually strange or was it my panic that made it sound odd? At the time I was sure he sounded more zombie than human. I ran to my house as fast as my middle-aged body could manage.

The next morning dawned clear and crisp. It was one of those beautiful London days that makes visitors and expatriates wonder why the city has such a poor reputation for weather. Once I'd had my little breakfast of old bread with a bit of government cheese, I made my way over to Patrick's house.

He was convinced that the driver was a zombie. "Mate, that man was infected. Why would he be driving like that, so out of his fucking mind?"

He seemed incredulous that I had any doubt. "We've got to start barricading the street at night, cause that wanker is just the tip of the iceberg—you can be sure that they are coming now. They must have run out of victims in the city proper."

So, we did just that. We got a bunch of the remaining adults on the block to start moving heavy objects towards both ends of our street. There was some disagreement about the necessity of the barricades, but when I shared my story about the crash (and the news of it spread among the neighbors), people came around to the idea. It was decided, though, that we would not fully seal the ends of the street. Old cars would block the middle of the entrances and they could be moved to let in friendly vehicles. We all knew the real danger was in the dark overnight hours, so we set up a revolving schedule of people who would guard the entrances from sundown to sun-up. It was agreed the older volunteers would take the early shifts, and that all shifts would include at least one younger adult, with a minimum of two people at each end of the street.

There were guns in several homes on the street, so it was also agreed that every team would have one gun, and that one of the two volunteers would know how to fire it. Because there was still an official ban, the guns had to be hidden in the bushes or under a parked car in the event of a military or police check-in. The volunteers settled on not wearing any shiny objects. The final part of the plan was to have bullhorns on either end of the street to be used for alarm purposes. One blast from the horn meant the guards were suspicious of something, two blasts meant there was possible trouble and repeated, ongoing blasts meant immediate danger.

After this was settled, some people voiced concerns about how the military or the police would react once they discovered what we were doing. Because their presence in recent weeks had dwindled to almost nothing, people felt police and military authority over these matters had eroded. The residents believed stories about military forces concentrated in the wealthy neighbor-hoods, the financial district and in government buildings. It was a theory in concurrence with the deep class divisions Brits internalized from birth. On the initial day of preparation, the volunteers seemed almost elated. We were finally acting, doing something after weeks of sitting around in fear, waiting. When Patrick and I discussed the plan at the end of the day, it was clear that there were serious flaws. The rear flanks through our gardens were unprotected because the streets that bordered ours were effectively unguarded. (We did visit the adjoining streets to see if their residents would adopt a similar defense plan). The zombies could walk through their yards into our backyards unmolested. And, if there was any kind of coordinated attack by infected people, our guards would be overwhelmed in a matter of seconds. The good news was that the disease, from all appearances, did not engender much camaraderie amongst the infected. They generally acted alone without a mind to their legion's feelings.

We sensed the virus spreading like rings from the city center. With young children and the elderly mostly gone, the street was ghostlike, even during the day. The teenage situation was less uniform. Without access to social media, teenagers got on with what was left in their lives. This was in part because they were needed in a way they had not been just weeks before. Some of them were tasked with caring for younger siblings in the country (or helping with elderly relatives) and others with readying for the defense of the neighborhood. Patrick's girls were in the former group and had left with Dawn to help care for their grandparents.

As the days passed and England's underrated mild summer turned into a wet, dreary fall, the circle closed in. Who could say what this unfolding horror really was? I thought about it as a power grab, letting the poor and defenseless kill each other in a rampage of blood while the elites sat protected in their towers and waited. For them it would be an earth with similar resources and many fewer people. Whatever the case, there would be a reckoning for the unblessed.

The first shudder of real panic and direct violence in Hillingdon started innocuously enough with people's pets. In early October as the lessening daylight faded into London's long northern evenings, cats and dogs began to go missing. Some were later found disembowelled in back alleys. I used to hear, before the silence of the virus nights fully set in, animal sounds that would wake me from a dead sleep. I never really knew what they were—maybe an animal in heat, perhaps two fighting. It was hard to tell coming out of a dream state. Even in the monolithic, car-humming suburbs, civilization is a thin, temporary bulwark against the eventual return to wildness. I assumed the animal sounds were cries of pets in the throes of terror and death. These pacified beasts were meeting their end by the species who had bred them and brought them to this earth. What we did not really know was whether these were zombie attacks, or simply hungry people hunting for meat in the safety of darkness. People began keeping their animals inside at night.

Rumors began to spread that Ealing, a gentrified borough just east of Hillingdon, had suffered a series of attacks on humans. The remaining neighbors gathered in a small huddle in the middle of the street. Schemes were constructed to put more people on guard duty (although no one seemed eager to sign up) and vitriol was thrown at the absent government and police, all of which struck me as predictable and useless. I was oddly comforted by the thought that we were now getting together in a way that would have been unthinkable prior to prepping for the flesh eaters. Other than an airing of grievances, nothing much was accomplished. We did agree to take an inventory of our guns, to keep the remaining teenagers inside after dark and to increase the number of guards at each end of the street to three. The only problem with the last part of the plan was that we did not have enough ambulatory people who fit the bill of security personnel. Many of the residents were out of shape, too terrified to act or both.

On October 15th, things began to get hairy. I had just returned to my semi-detached after being on watch with Patrick from six to midnight. We'd seen and heard little. The night was cold with a stiff wind. We kept warm by jogging in place and blowing into our hands. At one point we thought we heard a distant cry, although neither of us was sure it was anything beyond the wind.

I was woken from a deep sleep by a high-pitched screeching, which I initially took as part of a nightmare I was having about wrestling a loaf of bread out of a toddler's hands at the local grocery store. When I grabbed the bread, the toddler let out a blood-thinning scream. Just as his mother started to come at me brandishing a large zucchini, I realized the scream was coming from the street. I was in a waking nightmare. The screech came again and this time it was clear it was a human voice. I thought I might puke or piss my pants as I swung my legs out of bed. I heard the clamor of neighbors' voices on the street. I got my shit together and ran down the stairs, grabbing my coat and modified club.

People were running pell-mell and yelling as they went. The action was happening at the barricade on the south entrance to the street. The screaming got louder as I moved towards the source of the commotion. Approaching the large crowd of people, it was evident that something had gone very wrong. I pushed through the gathering circle. The screaming had transitioned to muted weeping sounds. The scene at the center of the group was ghastly. What looked to be a young teenage girl was lying on the ground with a gaping, bloody hole in her gut. Her face and hair were a dishevelled mess. She was gasping for breath. She could not speak, but was mouthing the words, "Help me," over and over.

There was a space of about ten to fifteen feet between her and the throng. People were yelling to stay back; it was clear she was infected. Sydney, who lived directly across the street from me, held his right hand to his face as he wept and an old-fashioned hunting shotgun in his left. People put their arms around him for support, but he could not stop sobbing.

And so it began. The tightening noose had reached our street. As the days grew darker and shorter the horror upon us was no longer a rumor. The screams we now heard at night were people being killed or people killing the zombies. Just as the wave crested into the outer suburbs, the food started to run out. This led to fewer people living on the street, as more people fled to the countryside, looking for a way out.

I'm not sure why I've stayed. It may be stubbornness. Perhaps it's the realization that the countryside may not be any better. There is not much news flowing from that direction, but I cannot imagine there being enough resources to deal with the new migrants. I also suspect the reckoning is coming now or later and must be faced regardless.

We have not seen any authorities for weeks and there are only about fifteen of us left "protecting" the street. Patrick is among them. When his family left, he told Dawn he'd meet her in a week or two; I don't think either of them believed it. I'm not sure what we are protecting. Are we serving as a bulwark against the coming hoard to slow their progress out of London? If the stories we've been hearing are true, our chances seem slim.

I've begun to lose track of the days. I find myself dozing off at odd hours when I'm in my house. It feels like it's always dark or getting dark. Suspected zombie incursions into our neighborhood are becoming a nightly occurrence. We are all up most of the night and try to sleep a bit during the day. Last night we heard hair-raising sounds from the next street over. A group of us moved into Patrick's back garden (which faced the direction of the noise) with homemade weapons and vintage shotguns in hand. Patrick had an old pistol. From what we could tell there was a full-on melee taking place. There were frantic cries for help and what sounded like the tearing of flesh, then silence.

It's been raining most of the day today. I took a daytime shift at the northern street barricade and then headed back to eat some of the canned soup we've been living on for the past couple of weeks. There was talk of further government food drops into the suburbs, but we've not seen anything yet. If they don't come soon, it'll be down to hunting squirrels and foxes for meat.

Helicopters are flying overhead right now, heading towards the city center. These flights have increased in frequency over the past couple of days. I am suspicious these flights are ferrying the rich and royals out of their mansions and palaces. There is no way of confirming this, but how else would a class-based society deal with the apocalypse? Even if these flights are a sign of an ongoing betrayal, I still feel a sense of relief as they fly by. May be a weakness on my part. More likely I've internalized the part I play in the hierarchy.

The water has stopped running. We have teams carrying water from a nearby stream. The trip, less than a half mile away, is not for the faint of heart. We've seen mangled bodies in the bordering woods.

We are getting very low on supplies. We are starting to look like the zombies. None of my pants fit anymore. I think we may have to abandon our little project and take our chances in the country.

I need to rest for bit now and take a break from writing.

Up again, what time is it? It's so dark.

Out of a dead sleep.

Did I hear something in the backyard? I need to look out the window.

Oh god, it's coming across the patio. Is it dragging something?
What the fuck is it?

SECTION SIX:
POEMS

BUDDY RICH

Rich in bed almost dead.

"Torme, play those bus tapes for me. I told those motherfuckers straight!
'Get your shit together boys or it's gonna be a long trip.'"

My father says, "Do you know what people miss as they lay dying?"

"Umm, not sure, the sounds of birds chirping?"

"No," he says, "their bodies, they miss using their bodies."

Poor Rich.
His clothes always fit tight over his monkey body,
like they could not contain his virility,
like he might burst the seams at any moment.
Mayer says Rich was a virtuoso,
one of the best technical musicians to have lived,
Horowitz's equal.

"His solos were stories that led through a universe, he kidnapped people."

Those drums made him fucking mad.
Everything made him mad.
He had to knock on them so he didn't bash more heads.
An instrument worth striking with fury.

Face red as a punch bowl, cheeks puffed out,
sweat pouring down his chin onto the skins,

CONTINUED...

holding his breath for an entire song lest something have the audacity to interrupt him. Only mortal drummers need breath.

Always first onto the snare, the rim shots, the speed,
a maniacal beast scowling like a petulant child,
sweltering into the groove.

Rich said, "It's a fucking instrument you don't just bang on it like a goddamn monkey unless that's what the music calls for."

Of course, at times it did.

FLY

What is that? A tsetse fly? I must admit I have no idea.
My ignorance astounds me.
I have become more ignorant as I age.
I thought it was supposed to be the opposite.

It's here on the bathroom wall deep inside this monolithic hospital building.
How the fuck did it get here?
This place is hermetically sealed.
I could barely get in.

Our insect brethren are obstinate about life.
We design fortresses to keep them out,
but still they persist, lounging by the urinal on this winter's day.
Maybe it's mockery not warmth they seek.

SKIN OF OUR TEETH

It's descriptive but hard to know for sure what it means.
If your teeth had skin, what would it look like?
Perhaps a dark pink like the inside of our mouths,
strung with veins pulsing, placenta-like,
in view, just below the surface.

If you happen to find yourself falling off a bridge and catch the railing by
your mouth, would this teeth skin give you better grip as you bore down on
the metal?
Would it stretch, holding fast for a moment, before you slipped away?

Sadness is like this, I think.
The chasm is there as we weep.
We know people are shut away who can't stop.
After all, who can take weeping for that long?

The sorrow of the world bests all high cards.
It mocks lovely summer, resplendent fall, snow on upturned faces.
Flouts the smell of babies, flowers, and dogs' armpits.
If we're not careful, all can be consumed.

We have to, as we can, hold on by the skin, by the teeth,
with whatever we can to meet another day.
With what strength there is in our bones,
we must fashion courage.

DOGS

Some dogs pull their masters through perilous blizzards,
others are trained to bite on demand,
still others run for hours in braying packs
hunting mammals for sport

This dog is not like that
She likes short walks when it is not too hot nor too cold
She's an excellent sleeper
She will not bound to you upon entry,
she may raise her head

She is small, but heavy
Her talent is placing her bones against your bones
When you are overcome, breathless with grief,
she leans in, pushing against you
waiting with patience for the maelstrom to pass

CPSIA information can be obtained
at www.ICGtesting.com
Printed in the USA
LVHW052318071122
732573LV00003B/550